MW01234145

MEDICAL WORKERS

J. P. Miller

Rourke
Educational Media

A Division of
Carson
Dellosa
Education.

Before Reading: *Building Background Knowledge and Vocabulary*

Building background knowledge can help children process new information and build upon what they already know. Before reading a book, it is important to tap into what children already know about the topic. This will help them develop their vocabulary and increase their reading comprehension.

Questions and Activities to Build Background Knowledge:

1. Look at the front cover of the book and read the title. What do you think this book will be about?
2. What do you already know about this topic?
3. Take a book walk and skim the pages. Look at the table of contents, photographs, captions, and bold words. Did these text features give you any information or predictions about what you will read in this book?

Vocabulary: *Vocabulary Is Key to Reading Comprehension*

Use the following directions to prompt a conversation about each word.

- Read the vocabulary words.
- What comes to mind when you see each word?
- What do you think each word means?

Vocabulary Words:
- diagnose
- environmental
- evacuation
- exercise
- surgeon
- refugees

During Reading: *Reading for Meaning and Understanding*

To achieve deep comprehension of a book, children are encouraged to use close reading strategies. During reading, it is important to have children stop and make connections. These connections result in deeper analysis and understanding of a book.

Close Reading a Text

During reading, have children stop and talk about the following:

- Any confusing parts
- Any unknown words
- Text to text, text to self, text to world connections
- The main idea in each chapter or heading

Encourage children to use context clues to determine the meaning of any unknown words. These strategies will help children learn to analyze the text more thoroughly as they read.

When you are finished reading this book, turn to the next-to-last page for **After-Reading Questions** and an **Activity**.

TABLE OF CONTENTS

THE IMPORTANCE OF MEDICAL WORKERS

A siren blares. The ambulance races to the military hospital. The ambulance is met by different Medical Workers. Each is ready to do their job: saving lives.

Medical Workers take care of members in all of the US Military branches: the Army, Air Force, Navy, Marines, and Coast Guard. They make sure military members are healthy enough to do their jobs.

Medical Workers are there on and off the battlefield. They give the physical exams that military members have each year. Some Medical Workers treat specific kinds of health issues. If a military doctor or nurse finds a health problem, the patient must then visit a special doctor or **surgeon**. They are usually military members too.

surgeon (SUR-juhn): a doctor who specializes in performing operations

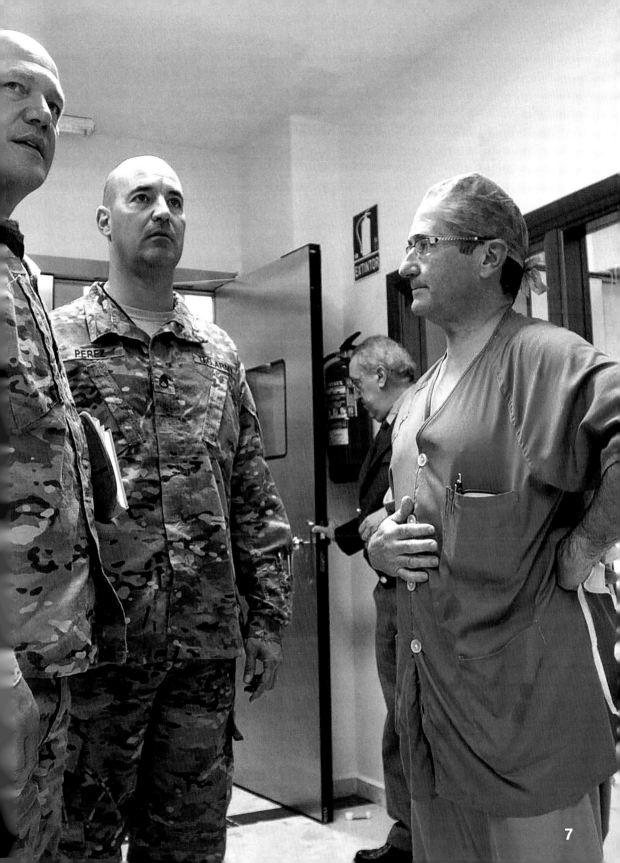

HEALING HANDS

Getting an injured person to safety sometimes takes more than an ambulance. Aeromedical **Evacuation** Teams use a special kind of plane called a KC-135 to fly patients long distances. They can quickly get patients to a hospital from areas where there are no hospitals. The planes have flight emergency rooms inside. The Aeromedical Evacuation Team has five members. The Aeromedical Evacuation Team does all the work of an emergency room team on the ground, but they do it in the air.

AIRCRAFT TRANSFORMED

During World War II, it took two or three weeks to move injured military members from the battlefield to safety. With the use of military medical aircraft such as C17s, C-130s, and KC-135s, they can now be moved to safety in 72 hours.

evacuation (i-VAK-yoo-aye-shuhn): to move away from an area or building because it is dangerous there

To do well as an Aeromedical Evacuation Specialist, it is important to be able to work under stress. You must have a lot of training. You also must be healthy enough to fly on a plane and move patients.

"You don't always know what to expect on a mission. That being said, you have to always plan one step ahead."
— Teresa Sullard, Senior Master Sergeant, US Air Force (Retired), Superintendent of Air Crew Training

Gunfire echoes over the fields and **refugees** cry for help. The scene looks frightening, but it is not real. A Medical Logistics Officer has helped set up an **exercise** to train Medical Workers and other military members. Actors and fake buildings make the base look and feel like a real foreign war zone. The Medical Logistics Officer has prepared for this for months. That means visiting the site, collecting information, and ordering supplies.

From these exercises, Medical Logistics Officers learn what doctors, nurses, and other medical staff need in battle. They make sure that the Medical Workers have the supplies and equipment needed to run base hospitals and other units. They use special computer programs to keep track of supplies and equipment.

exercise (EK-sur-size): something that you do in order to practice a skill

refugees (ref-yoo-JEEZ): people who are forced to leave their home or country to escape war, religious persecution, or natural disaster

The success of a military medical team depends on its Medical Logistics Officer. If they make the wrong decision, injured people might not get the medical care that they need. It is a stressful job. Medical Logistics Officers work long hours. They sometimes go a long time without seeing their families.

To do well as a Medical Logistics Officer, you must be good at organizing information. It is important to be able to make long-term plans. You must also be reliable.

"Half the battle is showing up where you are supposed to be with what you are supposed to have."
— Alan C. Schmitz, Captain, US Army, Medical Logistics Officer

A visit to a Military Doctor's office on a military base is often not very different from one in your local community. Military Doctors can have many different jobs. In times of peace, they work in clinics and even aboard ships. They give people yearly health exams and treat minor injuries. In times of war, Military Doctors work near battles to treat injured people there.

TWO CAREER PATHS

There are two ways to become a medical doctor in the military. One is to have earned a medical degree before entering the military. The other is to attend the Uniformed Services University of Health Sciences while serving in the military as a Second Lieutenant.

To be a successful as a military doctor, it is important to want to help others. You must pay attention to details and enjoy learning new things. You must also be able to make good decisions when you **diagnose** and treat your patients.

diagnose (dye-uhg-NOHS): to determine what disease a patient has or what the cause of a problem is

Dangerous illnesses such as COVID-19 can spread all around the world. That includes military bases and people in war zones too. How can military members stay safe? It is up to **Environmental** Health and Safety Specialists to protect them.

Environmental Health and Safety Specialists perform safety checks. They make sure that food is not spoiled, water is safe to drink, and buildings are safe. They make sure that people are following health and safety rules, such as wearing masks and cleaning surfaces as needed.

environmental (en-VYE-ruhn-MENT-uhl): related to the natural surroundings of living things

STOPPING THE VIRUS

To slow the spread of COVID-19, the US Military told many military members to stay home. They temporarily stopped recruiting and training people. They worked with Environmental Health and Safety Specialists to keep people safe.

To do well as an Environmental Health and Safety Specialist, you must be able to gather information. You should like science and enjoy learning new things. You must also be good at educating people about how to stay safe.

Environmental Health and Safety Specialists sometimes go into dangerous buildings or are around things that could make them sick. You must be okay with taking risks to keep other people safe.

SAFETY DETECTIVES

If someone on a military base has an accident, Environmental Health and Safety Specialists help determine how it happened. They gather all the facts and decide if there is a problem with equipment or buildings.

Military members must be healthy to do their jobs. That includes their minds too. Working in the military often means seeing and experiencing upsetting things. The job of Mental Health Workers is to ensure that the mental health of military members is good.

If a military member needs mental health help, Mental Health Workers can give them tests to find the problem. They work with other Medical Workers to discuss treatment options. They help the military member talk about their problems so they feel better. Sometimes, they help the military member get medication to help.

JUST A PHONE CALL AWAY

Some people have a difficult time asking for help. The Military Mental Health Program has a telephone help line to make it easier. Military members who need mental health help can call 24 hours a day.

To be a good Mental Health Worker, it is important to be a good listener. You must want to help others and like working with people. You must also like learning. Mental Health Workers attend 17 weeks of classes after basic training. Some Mental Health Workers have even more school after that!

LIFE OR DEATH DECISIONS

Medical Workers keep military members healthy, including their bodies and minds. They must be good at making decisions. Their choices can mean the difference between a patient living or dying.

Do you like to help people? Are you able to make good decisions quickly? If so, you might be a good Medical Worker!

MEMORY GAME

Look at the pictures. What do you remember reading on the pages where each image appeared?

INDEX

AFTER-READING QUESTIONS

1. How do military members get patients from one place to another quickly?

2. Why are military training exercises important?

3. What are three different kinds of jobs that Medical Workers have?

4. What things do Environmental Health and Safety Specialists check?

5. What can Mental Health Workers do to help their patients?

ACTIVITY

Make your own first aid kit! Using an old shoe box, cover the box and then the lid in construction paper. Draw and color in labels on the top and sides of your box. Fill the box with supplies to treat minor injuries. You might want to include cotton balls, adhesive bandages, rubber gloves, antibiotic ointment, first aid tape, and tweezers for splinters.

ABOUT THE AUTHOR

J. P. is a veteran of the United States Air Force living in Metro Atlanta, Georgia. She now writes children's books that augment a child's classroom experience. J. P. is very excited to combine her love for writing with her military experience to produce the *Careers in the US Military* series.

www.rourkeeducationalmedia.com

Quote sources: Teresa Sullard, interview by author. Alan C. Schmitz, interview by author.

PHOTO CREDITS: page 5: ©玄史生 / Wikimedia; page 7: ©Capt. Jeku Arce/U.S. Army / Wikimedia; page 9: ©Soumya Shaw / Wikimedia(background); page 9: ©Peterfz30 / Shutterstock(top); page 9: ©U.S. Air Force Photo/Master Sgt. Scott Reed / Wikimedia(bottom); page 11: ©Staff Sgt. Steve Lewis / U.S. Air Force; page 13: ©Tech Sgt. Peter Dean / U.S. Air Force; page 15: ©pingvin121674 / Shutterstock(background); page 15: ©Staff Sgt. Clay Lancaster / Wikimedia(top); page 15: ©LCpl. T. J. Kaemmere/DOD/ZUMA Press / Newscom(bottom); page 17: ©Airman Robert Brooks/U.S. Navy / Wikimedia; page 19: ©Africa Studio / Shutterstock(background); page 19: ©Senior Master Sgt. Ken Johnson / U.S. Air National Guard(top); page 19: ©Airman 1st Class Siuta B. Ika / U.S. Air Force(bottom); page 21: ©Sgt. James D. Sims/U.S. Army / Wikimedia; page 23: ©Russell Toof / U.S. Army; page 25: ©SDI Productions / Getty Images; page 27: ©Kimberly Gaither / U.S. Air Force; page 29: ©Sgt. Breanne Pye/U.S. Army / U.S. Department of Defense

Edited by: Tracie Santos
Cover and interior design by: Alison Tracey

Library of Congress PCN Data

Medical Workers / J. P. Miller
(Careers in the US Military)
ISBN 978-1-73164-353-7 (hard cover)(alk. paper)
ISBN 978-1-73164-317-9 (soft cover)
ISBN 978-1-73164-385-8 (e-Book)
ISBN 978-1-73164-417-6 (ePub)
Library of Congress Control Number: 2020945274

Rourke Educational Media
Printed in the United States of America
04-3082211948